There Was An Old Woman

RETOLD & DRAWN BY STEVEN KELLOGG

FOUR WINDS PRESS · NEW YORK

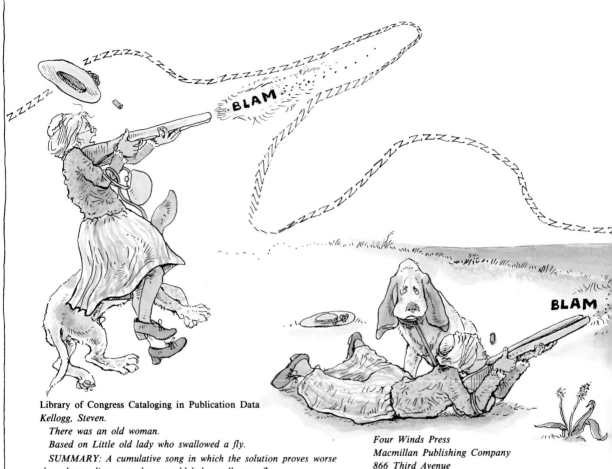

Library of Congress Cataloging in Publication Data
Kellogg, Steven.
  There was an old woman.
  Based on Little old lady who swallowed a fly.
  SUMMARY: A cumulative song in which the solution proves worse
than the predicament when an old lady swallows a fly.
  1. Folk-songs, English. [I. Folk songs, English] I. Little old lady who
swallowed a fly. II. Title.
[PZ8.3.K33Th 1980]   398'.8   80-15293   ISBN 0-02-749780-1
Copyright © 1974 by Steven Kellogg

Four Winds Press
Macmillan Publishing Company
866 Third Avenue
New York, NY 10022

Collier Macmillan Canada, Inc.
1200 Eglinton Avenue East
Suite 200
Don Mills, Ontario M3C 3N1
Printed in the United States of America
2 3 4 5 6 7 8 9 10

For Colin

I HATE flies!
YOUR BIG CHANCE
TO FIND
FAME
AND
FORTUNE
JOIN
THE

There was an old woman who swallowed a fly.
I wonder why
She swallowed a fly.
Poor old woman, she's sure to die.

There was an old woman who swallowed a spider
That wriggled and jiggled and wriggled inside her.
She swallowed the spider to catch the fly.
I wonder why
She swallowed a fly.
Poor old woman, she's sure to die.

There was an old woman who swallowed a bird.
How absurd
To swallow a bird.
She swallowed the bird to catch the spider
That wriggled and jiggled and wriggled inside her.
She swallowed the spider to catch the fly.
I wonder why
She swallowed a fly.
Poor old woman, she's sure to die.

There was an old woman who swallowed a cat.
Fancy that!
She swallowed a cat.
She swallowed the cat to catch the bird,
She swallowed the bird to catch the spider
That wriggled and jiggled and wriggled inside her.
She swallowed the spider to catch the fly.
I wonder why
She swallowed a fly.
Poor old woman, she's sure to die.

Meow.

There was an old woman who swallowed a dog.
She went the whole hog
And swallowed a dog.
She swallowed the dog to catch the cat,
She swallowed the cat to catch the bird,
She swallowed the bird to catch the spider
That wriggled and jiggled and wriggled inside her.
She swallowed the spider to catch the fly.
I wonder why
She swallowed a fly.
Poor old woman, she's sure to die.

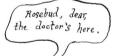

Rosebud, dear,
the doctor's here.

There was an old woman who swallowed a cow.

I wonder how

She swallowed a cow.

She swallowed the cow to catch the dog,

She swallowed the dog to catch the cat,

She swallowed the cat to catch the bird,

She swallowed the bird to catch the spider

That wriggled and jiggled and wriggled inside her.

She swallowed the spider to catch the fly.

I wonder why

She swallowed a fly.

Poor old woman, she's sure to die.

Rosebud! Rosebud!
LUGG'S LOADS
TRUST YOUR LOAD TO: LARRY LUGG
OKay. Hop in back.
Going my way, Mac?
FAME

There was an old woman
Who swallowed a horse . . .

She died of course!